This book is a work of fiction. Any resemblance to actual persons, living or dead, or actual events is purely coincidental.

Illustrations by Linnea Thurston.

Published by Q & A Publishing LLC.

For information, contact https://amazom.com/author/linnea.adrienne

Printed in the United States of America.

In a beautiful Californian coastal town, there was a large gathering at the beach. It was Beach Clean-up Day and the rangers had gathered the volunteers into groups.

Ranger Trish was just finishing up roll call of the Junior Rangers. 'Is L-L-Y-R here?' she asked.

"Here!" Llyr said raising his hand.

"How do you pronounce your name junior ranger?'

He smiled and said, 'just like ear with a L at the beginning.'

Llyr was an adventurous young boy. As a junior ranger, he was able to do what he loved, exploring and taking care of the animals that lived in and near the ocean.

Today was a very special day because Llyr and some other junior rangers were going on their first community beach clean-up mission. They wanted to make sure the ocean and beach stayed clean and safe for all the creatures it called home.

The children ran to their section of the beach with their bags for collecting trash.

As they were picking up trash, the junior scouts heard a crying sound just beyond some rocks and sand dunes.

It was a scared and perhaps injured little elephant seal pup!

The poor pup was tangled in trash and struggling to flop or galumph to his mother, who was waiting for him in the distance towards the water.

Llyr's heart filled with sadness and determination.

He knew he had to help the little seal pup get back to his mother.

He carefully approached the pup but kept some distance. He said to the pup "Don't worry little one. I'll help you!"

Llyr reminded everyone to keep some distance from the seal pup. He immediately ran to his mother.

She was also a ranger and he told her about the seal pup.

Llyr's mother knew they couldn't do it alone, so she called for help from Ranger Trish and the other rangers. They all rushed to the sand dune, ready to rescue the little seal pup and unite it with its mother.

Together, Llyr, his mother, and the other rangers worked tirelessly to free the seal pup from the tangles of trash.

The seal's mother looked on. The rangers knew she was worried about her baby and the people being so close to it.

Llyr shouted out to the momma elephant seal 'Don't worry momma, they are freeing your pup for you'.

The rangers used their special tools and gentle hands to carefully remove each piece of trash, making sure not to hurt the little pup.

With every piece of trash they removed, the seal pup squealed in joy and relief. He knew he was one step closer to being reunited with his loving mother.

Llyr and the rangers cheered for the little pup, encouraging him to stay strong.

Finally, the last piece of trash was removed. The seal pup was free!

He wiggled and waggled, showing his gratitude and excitement. He knew it was time to join his mother.

With gentle guiding, Llyr and the rangers guided the seal pup back towards the water and his mom.

The pup seal pup reached his mother, and they greeted each other with happy barks and kisses.

Llyr watched with a big smile on his face, knowing that he and all the Rangers had helped save a life.

The hearts of all involved were filled with joy. They knew they had made a difference in the lives of these precious animals.

As Llyr, his mother and the rangers walked back to the ranger station, they couldn't help but feel proud of what they had accomplished.

The volunteers had not only cleaned up the beach, but everyone had also saved a beautiful creature and brought a family back together.

From that day on, Llyr became known as the little hero of the Elephant Seal pups. He continued to protect and care for all the animals and birds, making sure their homes were clean and safe.

The other Junior Rangers followed his example, they were always ready to lend a helping hand.

And so, the adventures of Junior Ranger Llyr and his friends continued, making the world a better place for animals and humans alike.

They knew that with their love, teamwork and determination, they could make a difference.

The End

Made in the USA
Las Vegas, NV
08 September 2023

77246479R00026